A World of My Own

According to the wish of the author, this book is published in Britain by his great friend and publisher for many years Max Reinhardt, and in Canada by his niece and publisher Louise Dennys. —*YC*

A WORLD OF MY OWN

A Dream Diary

GRAHAM GREENE

VIKING

VIKING
Published by the Penguin Group
Penguin Books USA Inc., 375 Hudson Street,
New York, New York 10014, U.S.A.
Penguin Books Ltd, 27 Wrights Lane,
London W8 5TZ, England
Penguin Books Australia Ltd, Ringwood,
Victoria, Australia
Penguin Books Canada Ltd, 10 Alcorn Avenue,
Toronto, Ontario, Canada M4V 3B2
Penguin Books (N.Z.) Ltd, 182-190 Wairau Road,
Auckland 10, New Zealand

Penguin Books Ltd, Registered Offices:
Harmondsworth, Middlesex, England

First published in 1994 by Viking Penguin,
a division of Penguin Books USA Inc.

1 3 5 7 9 10 8 6 4 2

LIBRARY OF CONGRESS CATALOGING IN PUBLICATION DATA

Greene, Graham
A world of my own : a dream diary / Graham Greene.
p. cm.
ISBN 0-670-85279-1
1. Greene, Graham—Diaries. 2. Novelists,
English—20th century—Diaries. 3. Dreams. I. Title.
PR6013.R44Z476 1994
828´.91203—dc20   94-9945

Printed in the United States of America

Foreword

A few days before he died, when his daughter, Caroline, and I were with him at L'Hôpital de la Providence in Vevey, Graham Greene asked me to prepare this dream diary for publication. Only a strong desire to keep a promise made to him induces me, therefore, to write a modest foreword to this posthumous book he entitled *A World of My Own*.

Graham guarded his privacy as fiercely as he respected the privacy of others. He always refused to write an autobiography—after he had 'closed the record at the age of about twenty-seven' with *A Sort of Life*—because, as he said, it would have inevitably involved incursions into the privacy of other people's lives. The private world of his dreams, however, was one that he nurtured carefully, recording it almost daily in the dream diaries that he kept over the last twenty-five years.

From those several volumes, he made this small

selection for public reading, choosing carefully and deliberately. The project engaged him in the last months of his life. It interested him. And one of the pleasures of this book is the pleasure that he himself clearly took in making the selection.

In this world of the subconscious and the imagination—a world *farfelu* as he used to call it—where everything intersects and gets tangled up beyond time, Graham obviously feels at ease and happy. 'In a sense it is an autobiography,' he says in his Introduction; and it's true that between the secret world of dreams and the real world he lived in the divide is narrow. And the barriers have been lifted. Here he can gossip about others, or give free rein to his eagerness for adventure or his delight in the absurd. Dreaming was like taking a holiday from himself. As he confided to a friend: 'If one can remember an entire dream, the result is a sense of entertainment sufficiently marked to give one the illusion of being catapulted into a different world. One finds oneself remote from one's conscious preoccupations.'

I told him once that I was astonished by the clarity with which he remembered his dreams, the preciseness of detail he retained. He explained that the habit of remembering went back to the time he first kept a dream diary—when, as a boy, he underwent psychoanalysis and was required by his analyst to retell his dreams (sometimes with embarrassing results—as when he had to confess to an erotic dream about his analyst's beautiful wife). Later, when he again began to keep a dream diary, he always had a pencil and paper at hand on his bedside table so that when he awoke from a dream, which happened on average four or five times a night, he could jot down key words that in the morning would allow him to reconstruct it. He would then transcribe it into his diary. I remember the very first diary that he had—a large notebook of dark green leather, given to him by friends. Another was the colour of Bordeaux wine.

It is well known that Graham was always very interested in dreams, and that he relied a great deal on the role played by the subconscious in writing. He would sit down to work straightway after breakfast, writing until he had five hundred words (which in the last while he reduced to approximately two hundred). He was in the habit of then rereading, every evening before going to bed, the section of the novel or story he had written in the morning, leaving his subconscious to work during the night. Some dreams enabled him to overcome a 'blockage'; others provided him on occasion with material for short stories or even an idea for a new novel (as with *It's a Battlefield*, and *The Honorary Consul*). Sometimes, as he wrote, 'identification with a character goes so far that one may dream his dream and not one's own'—as happened during the writing of *A Burnt-Out Case*, so that he was able to attribute his own dream to his character Querry and so extricate himself from an impasse in the narrative.

The most startling aspect of his dreams was their warning nature. One day, I remember, he appeared looking terribly upset. When I enquired after the reason for that distress, he replied: 'I dreamt of a catastrophe. I hope nothing has happened to one of my family or a close friend.' A few hours later we heard on the radio that a plane had crashed into the sea between Corsica and Nice, only a few miles away from his flat in Antibes, killing, I believe, all on board. One of the passengers on the flight was General Cogny, whom Graham knew well from his days in Vietnam.

Examples of that kind are numerous. Visions of panic and distress, visions of happiness—the impressions left in his mind by a dream were so vivid, so clear in every detail, that they would sometimes pursue him and influence his mood for hours after he awakened.

Today, remembering, I can't help thinking about a persistent dream of his which, like a kind of riddle, now seems to have sheltered a personal message. In

A Sort of Life he refers to a series of dreams which recurred over the years after the death of his father in 1943, and he writes: 'In them my father was always shut away in hospital out of touch with his wife and children—though sometimes he returned home on a visit, a silent solitary man, not really cured, who would have to go back again into exile. The dreams remain vivid even today, so that sometimes it is an effort for me to realize that there was no hospital, no separation and that he lived with my mother till he died.' His unhappiness at these frequent returns to the hospital is perhaps just coincidence, but it is difficult not to see in the dreams a premonition of what he himself would have to endure, nearly half a century later, at the end of his life—his own enforced exiles in hospital, which he suffered from so much.

In this last book of his, he gives us a glimpse of the strenuous inner life, his elusive source of creativity, that lay beyond that door which he always kept firmly closed, for fear an intruder might destroy 'the pattern in the carpet'. As a kind of farewell, Graham opens a door for us on the world of his own.

Graham—

In *The Power and the Glory* you wrote: 'The glittering worlds lay there in space like a promise; the world was not the universe. Somewhere Christ might not have died.'

If such a place exists, you certainly have found it.

Yvonne Cloetta
Vevey, Switzerland
October 1991

Contents

Contents

The waking have one world in common,
but the sleeping turn aside each
into a world of his own.

HERACLITUS OF EPHESUS

500 BC

Introduction

It can be a comfort sometimes to know that there is a world which is purely one's own—the experience in that world, of travel, danger, happiness, is shared with no one else. There are no witnesses. No libel actions. The characters I meet there have no memory of meeting me, no journalist or would-be biographer can check my account with another's. I can hardly be prosecuted under the Official Secrets Act for any incident connected with the security services. I *have* spoken with Khrushchev at a dinner party, I *have* been sent by the Secret Service to murder Goebbels. I am not lying—and yet, of all the witnesses who share these scenes with me, there is not one who can claim from his personal knowledge that what I describe is untrue.

I decided to choose, out of a diary of more than eight hundred pages, begun in 1965 and ended in 1989, selected scenes from My Own World. In a

sense it is an autobiography, beginning with Happiness and ending with Death, of a rather bizarre life
during the last third of a century (the wars described
here belong to the sixties, not the forties)—but no
biographer will care to make use of it, even though
I may sometimes include a date when I want to give
for my own satisfaction the day and the year when
an unusual event or an unusual meeting took place.

For that reason I thought at first of beginning with
my unexpected encounter with Henry James on a
river boat in Bolivia in the spring of 1988. However,
my plan to begin with this strange episode changed
when in January 1989 I experienced for the first
time, in all the records which I have kept of this
private world for more than twenty years, happiness.
Great names are a commonplace in this World of
My Own, but real meaningless and inexplicable
happiness—this is the only experience of it I have
recorded.

It has often been suggested that opium helps to
open the closed door of this World, but I have no
evidence for this. In the fifties, when I was smoking
opium in Vietnam and Malaya, I was busy keeping
a diary of violent events in the Common World, but
I have in my memory only one remarkable happening in the World of My Own, remarkable because it
goes so far back in time—in fact to the year 1 AD.

I was living then not far from Bethlehem, and I

decided to walk down to that small town to visit a brothel I knew there, carrying a gold coin with which to pay the girl whom I would choose. At the approach to the town I saw a strange sight: a group of men in Eastern clothes who were bowing and offering gifts. To what? To a blank wall. There was no one there to receive their gifts or return their salutation. I stood quite a while watching this curious scene and then something—I don't know what—impelled me to throw my gold coin at the wall and turn away.

Time in the World of One's Own can move slowly or it can move very rapidly. In this case the centuries passed by me like a flash and I found myself lying on my bed reading in the New Testament a story of how some Eastern kings came to a stable in Bethlehem, and I realized that this was what I had seen. My first thought was: 'Well, I went to Bethlehem to give that gold coin to a woman and it seems that I did in fact give it to a woman, even though all I saw was a blank wall.'

There is an imaginative side to the World of One's Own quite distinct from that of the Common World. Robert Louis Stevenson told an interviewer about the strange case of Dr Jekyll and Mr Hyde: 'On one occasion I was very hard up for money and I felt I had to do something. I thought and thought, and tried hard to find a subject to write about. At night

I dreamt the story, it practically came to me as a gift, and what makes it appear more odd is that I was quite in the habit of dreaming stories. Thus, not long ago, I dreamt the story of "Olalla", and I have at the present moment two unwritten stories I likewise dreamt.'

'Olalla' is an unfairly neglected story of Stevenson's and in it there is a kind of underground resemblance to Dr Jekyll. It is a story which belongs quite definitely to the World of His Own rather than to Spain, where the scene is supposed to be set, just as in Dr Jekyll's London we seem to be moving in the streets of Edinburgh or the streets of a city in Stevenson's own private world.

The strange thing is that the author, when he is in the Common World, feels a stranger in the World of His Own, and Stevenson was lost and puzzled by his own story. He wrote a letter: 'The trouble with "Olalla" is that it somehow sounds false . . . the odd problem is: what makes a story true? "Markheim" is true; "Olalla" false, and I don't know why.' He even went so far, in the case of Dr Jekyll, as to throw the first draft into the fire.

A few of my short stories have been drawn from memories of the World of My Own. In 'Dream of a Strange Land' I recorded my experience in that World when I was a leper seeking treatment in Swe-

den. Only the sound of a shot with which the printed
tale ends has been added. In another story, 'The
Root of All Evil', laid in Germany far back in the
nineteenth century, I changed nothing after I woke,
with a smile of amusement, from My Own World to
the Common World.

There is another side to what we call dreams, very
interestingly exposed in J.W. Dunne's *Experiment
with Time*. They contain scraps of the future as well
as of the past. I have already written of how at the
age of seven I dreamed of a shipwreck on the night
the *Titanic* went down, and again nine years later I
witnessed another disastrous shipwreck in the Irish
Sea. As I look through the long record of my dreams
I note time and again incidents of the Common
World that have occurred a few days after the
dream. They are too trivial to include here, but I am
convinced that Dunne was right.

The strangeness of my completely unexpected
meeting with Henry James in My Own World at
least seems worthy to take precedence in the second
chapter, to which I have given the title 'Some Fa-
mous Writers I Have Known'. Unlike the biographer, I do not find it necessary to plod along in the
footsteps of the years, and my earlier meeting with
Pope John Paul II in a hotel bedroom seems unimportant compared with my more recent meeting

with Henry James. (I am sure no good would have come to either the Pope or myself if I had woken him up. We were not made to like each other.)

The erotic side of life may seem oddly absent from this record but I do not wish to involve those whom I have loved in this World of My Own, even though I am powerless to censor biographers and journalists who write of them in the Common World. Another thing lacking is nightmare. Wars and danger are here, but nothing as bad as the witch who used to haunt a passage on the way to the nursery at home when I was a child until at last I turned and faced her and she disappeared for ever. I have known fear often enough in Haiti and Vietnam in My Own World, but never terror, never nightmare. Perhaps there has always been an element of adventure and a kind of pleasure in my fear, both in the Common World and in the World of My Own.

A World of My Own

I

Happiness

It was 1965. I had decided to do a little Liberal canvassing in a forthcoming by-election and I had chosen a country town called Horden. Apparently one couldn't leave from the main station at Victoria, but by a branch line, the Horden line, which had its own entrance. I gathered that it was a very old and very interesting line and so it proved.

The first train to leave consisted of pretty carriages which must have dated back more than a hundred years, but this train didn't go to Horden. The second train was bound there, but it was very crowded. I was much struck by the kindness and jollity of the passengers, who welcomed me and made room for me in a very packed carriage. They all wore strange clothes—Edwardian or Victorian—and I was fascinated by the stations we passed. On one wide platform children were playing with scarlet balloons; another station was built like a ruined Greek temple;

at one point the track narrowed and the train went through a kind of tunnel made with mattresses.

I had never in my life felt such a sensation of happiness. Lights were beginning to come out in the quaint houses which we passed, and I longed to return with the woman I loved at just this hour of the evening.

The train drew up by a little antique shop and I heard a passenger say, 'You see, all the men are drinking or playing cards.'

A young couple (the girl pretty but quite unerotic and her husband a simple good-looking man with curly hair and an open face) became almost instantaneously like old friends. I said, 'I've lived in London fifty years and yet I've never heard before of the Horden line. I could make this journey every day and not be tired of it.'

The girl replied, 'The only thing is—don't let them put you up in a hostel if you stay the night.'

'Aren't there hotels?'

'They are just as bad.'

I had decided to do nothing about my canvassing. All I longed for was to see Horden. I had planned to be back in London for dinner, but all the same I enquired about a late train when I got out. I was a little apprehensive that it might have already left and I would find myself staying in a disagreeable hostel. However all was well, there was a late train at 10.25.

The girl took my hand and told me she would show me the town. I said, 'First the two of you will have a drink with me.' I could see the bars were full of laughing people. 'You are not teetotallers?' I asked.

'No,' the girl said.

'Then you choose the nicest pub.'

All the time there stayed with me that sense of inexplicable happiness. If only I could go back one day to the little town of Horden which exists in My Own World, but not in the world I share.

II

Some Famous Writers
I Have Known

An odd thing about this World of My Own is that it contains no living writers. It seems that a writer whom I have the pleasure of knowing must die before he enters my secret world.

Henry James

On April 28, 1988, I found myself on a most disagreeable river trip to Bogotá in the company of Henry James. The boat left after midnight and we had to find our way along the quay in complete darkness, carrying our hand baggage. I would have turned back if it had not been for the determination of the great author, and my admiration for his work.

What made things worse was the loud voice of an official—invisible in the darkness—who was continually shouting threats. 'Anyone who tries to come on board without a ticket will be fined one thousand dollars.' In the crowd pushing to get onto the boat it was impossible even to show our tickets.

There was no place to sit—we just managed to squeeze ourselves into a corridor tightly packed, mainly by women—but I heard no complaint from Henry James. At some place on the river the boat stopped for a few minutes and a few passengers got off. Surely, I urged James, we could take the opportunity and escape too, but no, James wouldn't hear of it. We must go on to the bitter end. 'For scientific reasons,' he told me.

Robert Graves

One night I had a happy encounter by the roadside with Robert Graves, who looked as young as when I had known him in the Common World when he lived near Oxford in 1923. He was pleased to see me again and recalled a chance meeting we had once had on the Italian frontier, which I had forgotten. I told him how much I had always admired his poems, even in the twenties, and how I still treasured a copy of his first poems, *Over the Brazier*.

'Do you remember,' I asked him, 'my own awful book of verse, *Babbling April*, about which you were kind in the case of one poem?' I teasingly added,

'Now the book is fetching even a higher price at auction than your own first book.'

Jean Cocteau

In November 1983 I met Jean Cocteau at a party and was pleasantly surprised. As I told him frankly, I expected to find his eyes cold, but they were understanding, even affectionate. His boyfriend turned up a little later dead drunk.

Ford Madox Ford

Talking to Ford Madox Ford I wanted to express my admiration for one of his books, which concerned the Spanish Civil War. He said he had never written such a book. Searching in vain for the title, I went to my bookshelves to find a book of his which might list the other. I found only two volumes in the Bodley Head edition—one a book of essays which I didn't know at all. His other titles were not given. Suddenly (several times I had begun to say *For Whom the Bell* . . . but checked myself) the title came to me—*Some Do Not*.

We went for a very pretty country walk together.

He told me of a legend that the Holy Virgin, standing on a hill, had bent down and picked out of the river we were passing a man who was drowning seven miles away from her.

'But the land is quite flat,' I said.

'Not if you look closer. It slopes down past that old millhouse to the lock.' People had spoken to me of the woman who kept the lock—a wonderful cook with a great interest in local history, which she tried to pass on to her sons.

We began to cross a field—nervously on my part, because it contained one large bull and a young one that showed itself too interested in our movements. I edged back on the road and, looking round, I saw the young bull had mounted on Ford's shoulders. He didn't seem disturbed.

I walked on to the lock to wait for him. There was a delicious smell of cooking and the woman was talking to a neighbour. The lock was just at the entrance to a small town. Ford joined me. The woman said she recommended soup and fish. We said we would go into the town and buy a bottle of wine. She offered to send her son, who was dressed in a sort of smock like an old-time agricultural labourer, but we insisted on going. As we went Ford said to me, 'Have you noticed that men don't like wearing anything that comes below the knee?'

T.S. Eliot

I was working one day for a poetry competition and had written one line—'Beauty makes crime noble'—when I was interrupted by a criticism flung at me from behind by T.S. Eliot. 'What does that mean? How can crime be noble?' He had, I noticed, grown a moustache.

W.H. Auden and Evelyn Waugh

Rather strange circumstances brought the two writers together. I had been part of a group who had managed to beat a gang of guerrillas, but the chief of the gang, Wystan Auden, had escaped. He was hidden somewhere in the brushwood which we were carefully searching. I had armed myself with a kitchen knife, for he was the most dangerous of our enemies. Suddenly he broke cover and dashed into a nearby house. He had been shot by Evelyn Waugh and was bleeding from his wounds.

I followed him and stuck my kitchen knife into his side, but he seemed unhurt by my blow and began a literary discussion of which, strangely enough, I can remember nothing.

Next night I found myself at a party, again with Auden, and I do remember our conversation then. I expressed my preference for living in England rather than in the United States because English literature was far richer than American. Shakespeare made all other writers into dwarfs and there could be no jealousy among dwarfs. American literature, having no such giant, gave room for jealousy.

Auden replied that all the same he was content in America. Although he was no scientist, he held a position in the science faculty of the university. He gave an impression of lazy well-being, tilted back in his chair.

I said, 'It would be fun if you could discover one small scientific principle so that we could speak of "The Auden Digit".'

Our hostess now left us alone, saying, 'Help yourselves to drinks.' We both agreed that the larger the bottle of whisky, the easier it was to welcome her invitation.

D.H. Lawrence

It was the Duke of Marlborough who introduced me to D.H. Lawrence. I found him younger and better groomed than I had expected. He was quite friendly towards my work.

Sartre

I remember having a discussion with Sartre. I had made notes of various questions to ask him, and I tried to be very precise. I apologized for the badness of my French, which prevented me from being as precise as I wanted to be, and Sartre said kindly, 'You speak French very well, but,' he added, 'I don't understand a word you say.'

Then he became amiable and referred to a book of mine which Robert Laffont had published in France, the English title being *The Origin of Brighton Rock*. It was a reproduction of a childish manuscript in brown ink—a story with animal characters—and it was illustrated by Beatrix Potter. Sartre very much admired her drawings, but he said nothing of my writing.

Solzhenitsyn

I met Solzhenitsyn one day in 1976, with another man who was speaking of a new magazine he was planning, and I suggested he should ask Solzhenitsyn to contribute to the first six numbers. He replied very insultingly that he couldn't bear Solzhenitsyn's small eyes and his high hypocritical moral tone.

On another occasion I was giving a party for Solzhenitsyn, who seemed to be known more as a painter than as a novelist, in my apartment in Moscow, which was crowded with pictures even along the passages. He was late and I had my doubts whether he would be allowed to come. I had left the door ajar to show that we were not afraid. I wondered whether he would enjoy his visit because there were so many twittering ladies around.

A stocky man in a beard whom I recognized as a KGB type arrived at the door and I thought we were in for trouble, but then I saw that Solzhenitsyn was with him, very badly dressed. The bearded man had some children with him and, having delivered the painter, he turned to go downstairs. I ran after him, thinking it was politic, and asked him if he would like a cup of tea. He said no, but if his children could have some caramels. . . . I took them from a bag which I had bought a few days earlier for my grandchildren. Suddenly he began to show an interest in the pictures. 'They are so lovely,' he said, and for a moment I thought he was going to weep with longing and nostalgia. I took him along the passage and showed him more. I was looking for a large painting of Solzhenitsyn's to show him what a great painter

his prisoner was, but it had mysteriously vanished—
I could find only a small one. I deliberately did not
take him into a room which contained only Art
Nouveau.

Edgar Wallace

I met Edgar Wallace only once, at a party, and he
told me he preferred his Australian stories but they
were not a success because they offended English
readers. I asked him about his hardback rights and
he said that his publisher, Collins, was putting them
up to auction. As we left the party together he asked
me jokingly if I was responsible for the story going
around that he had had sexual relations with E.M.
Forster. I denied it and said I thought the true story
concerned his relations with Hamish Hamilton.

III

In the Secret Service

My experiences in M.I.6. in My Own World were far more interesting than the desk work which I performed during three years in the Common World. Curiously enough, of the dozen or so characters I knew then only a couple found their way into the world I am writing of now. So perhaps the Official Secrets Act did cast its shadow even there. Of my experiences perhaps the most adventurous, and more in the spirit of the CIA than of M.I.6., was a certain mission to Germany.

I remember entering a richly furnished drawing-room where Goebbels was sitting in a gilt armchair. There were several other people in the room and I stood by a marble mantel waiting my opportunity, for I had with me a secret weapon for killing Goebbels—a cigarette of which the fumes would be quickly fatal if inhaled.

I tried to stand close to my victim, holding my cigarette where the fumes would reach him, but I grew impatient and thrust the end of the cigarette up his nostril, then fled from the room. I hoped that the poison would act quickly, and that there would be a confusion which would delay pursuit.

The street was empty and I turned right—then, realizing that I might be seen from the windows, I came back, keeping too close to the wall to be visible, and turned left. I took several side streets, but I had to return to the main street because I had been instructed to go to the North Station and take a train. There were no soldiers or police in sight, but of course they might now be waiting ahead of me.

I was tempted to turn into a park where there were long empty vistas, but I obeyed orders and almost at once the station came in view—a small local station. Here I found my contact, and a train was already coming in. I took two tickets to the end of the line and realized too late that I had made a bad mistake, for the end of the line proved to be Wapping, and surely to take a ticket to Wapping betrayed me as a foreign agent. The frontier station was the station before Wapping, and I was certain that there we would be intercepted. However we must have passed safely through or I would not be alive now to tell the story.

෨

Somehow I learnt of some new material concerning Kim Philby. Apparently he had recruited Ernest Hemingway to report on refugees from Hong Kong. Hemingway was very short of money and he earned in this way about five pounds a week, which he badly needed for his family.

෨

In 1980 I met the Russian ambassador at a large party. I spoke to him just before leaving and asked him if he would like to read a critical piece which I had written about M.I.6. He said he would. I had no sense of being a traitor—it seemed to me a good thing for both sides that he should read it.

෨

On one occasion I was catching a plane to Dakar, but there was some confusion at the airport when I had to send a telegram to the M.I.6. representative there announcing my arrival next morning. From Dakar I would be going on to Freetown in Sierra Leone, where Trevor Wilson, whom I had known in the last world war and also in Vietnam, was our representative. I happened to overhear a crossed line on the telephone. Some official was asking for a photo of me—apparently the Chinese Press Bureau could supply one. 'They'll make me look like a Chinaman,' I thought to reassure myself.

∽

In London I had been working with others in a large room resembling my old sub-editors' room at *The Times*. I was investigating a double agent who seemed to be connected with a German spy called Serge. I was told that the head of M.I.6. was particularly interested in the case and I felt a certain pride in telephoning him directly in front of my colleagues.

My immediate superior, who much resembled George Anderson, the chief home sub-editor on *The Times* in my days there in the twenties, told me, 'I doubt whether he'll speak to you. He's just ordered his glass of port.' But speak to me C did, beginning the conversation by exclaiming at what libellous articles had appeared in two weeklies, the *Spectator* and the *New Statesman*, the week before. 'We'll sue unless they can prove their facts,' I said, 'and this week too.'

C then came down to see me—a trim, amiable little man with a monocle. One of my colleagues— who closely resembled Colonel Maude, who had been assistant chief sub-editor when I was on *The Times*—joined in our talk. I recounted how this week the *New Statesman* had printed that the former C had left top secret information addressed to the head of the Foreign Office lying on his desk for anyone to read.

∽

In June 1965 I found myself back in West Africa for the Secret Service. At a railway station my bags were stolen by an African whom I had mistaken for a porter. I went to see the English stationmaster—a typical colonial type—in his office. 'Can I speak to you?' I asked and he replied rudely, 'Not now.'

I became angry and insisted. I knew he disliked me because of my undefined position in the colony. An African was brought before me, dressed in a long white robe, and I said he was certainly not the thief. The man had been travelling by the same train and

I asked him if he had seen anything. At that moment I saw out of the corner of my eye someone with the same striped shirt that the thief had worn.

'This is the man,' I said, but when he turned his face I saw that he was a wizened white man.

၈

Later that year I was working in Turkey for M.I.6. and I found myself in serious trouble. I had asked for an increase in salary and this had led to a long inquisition. It had begun discreetly enough when they wanted to know how much a year I spent on drinks. As I got all my drinks duty free at airports I couldn't produce a figure higher than two hundred pounds, which, I think, they regarded with suspicion.

A new man, a General Gates, arrived in uniform from London and started going the rounds of the big lounge in which we sat, introducing himself. My mistress was with me, looking very pretty, wearing an expensive fur jacket. I said, 'It's not a question of wasting money—I could earn much more if I got out of the Service and went home.'

I felt myself under suspicion of treachery. The general reached me on his rounds and coldly extended two fingers. He said he was going to read us a list of people in the organization who had proved unsatisfactory.

As a deliberate act of defiance I began to walk away, but I saw that my mistress remained talking to one of my colleagues. It seemed strange to me that the general was going to speak in her presence. I suspected that he had assumed she was my wife and had been thoroughly vetted.

A woman stopped me. 'Where are you going?'

'Shopping.'

I saw the woman looking with suspicion at my mistress's face. She was probably wondering whether I could afford such a mistress on my salary. She said, 'We've received a message from Egypt. They want you there because of your knowledge of Cairo.'

'That's absurd,' I said. 'I don't know anything of Cairo. I've only stopped off there once between planes.' I felt convinced when I looked at her that M.I.6 were planning to have me murdered there.

I decided to ask for political asylum in Turkey and I went to the immigration authorities. They refused to help me, but I told them to think again, and I showed them evidence I had of a bribe of five hundred pounds which had been taken by the head of their service.

All seemed to settle down and I was sent on to a French tropical town as an M.I.6. officer to join another officer. A senior officer whom I will call M had just come on another tour of inspection. I rather unkindly described him to my colleague as an obvious Secret Service type—'a cross between a foxy businessman and a major.'

As usual much of one's work consisted of giving an impression of work, and M was suitably impressed. We spent most of our time in the hotel. Someone there raised a hand in greeting. This gave me an opportunity. I told M, 'He's in the colonial administration. I knew him in Saigon.'

'Was he one of our agents?'

'I think he was.'

I went on to say that he might be useful for getting details of constructions in the town.

'Are the French building the place up?' he asked and I suggested we should take an evening drive together and see something of the European quarter, which was called Jiwena.

$\backsim$

On another occasion I was packing my things with the help of L, a friend in the same secret organization. I pointed out that I must take some very light clothes because I would be going nearly straight on from the States to Samoa on my mission. 'You'll have time for a shopping spree,' L said. I was proud at being given the mission and excited. At the air terminal I went up to the ticket counter and showed my ticket. 'Philadelphia 8.' I thought I saw a look of pity on the air hostess's face. Two men came up to me and asked for a lift to the airport. I sensed danger but I had no excuse to refuse them, and anyway I wanted to accept the challenge. They left the building with me, one walking on each side. Of what followed I have no memory.

∽

In January 1980 Kim Philby came to see me secretly in London. He was not as I remembered him—he was furtive and sharp-featured, and I was disappointed. He brought me an essay which he had written for the *Spectator* and I could honestly praise it. He had come from Havana by an English boat and I asked him whether he wasn't afraid of being arrested on the boat—but he gave me vaguely to understand that he was safe now. All the same, when he came to leave he readily accepted my offer to walk in front of him. There was one man in particular he had seen come out of a room into the corridor who was dangerous.

∽

With another man I was spying in Germany, dressed in the uniform of a German officer. We were very

light-hearted about the whole affair and to escape
we took a train that would cross the Swiss frontier.
Nor were we very perturbed when a beautiful young
woman demanded our papers. My companion, who
was of a higher rank, said that our papers were
packed in our luggage, and she accepted the excuse,
only marking our tickets in pencil with the numeral
75. Another moment of difficulty came at the frontier, where we had to show our passports—and we
had none. The chief passport officer was a pompous
fellow less manageable than the girl; however, his
rather ugly middle-aged wife proved to be on our
side, and the dominating partner. She simply told
him that the passports had already been examined.

～

My brother Raymond and I were carrying out espionage against the Nazis in Hamburg. We were
together in a hotel on the seventh floor when we
received a message from one of the employees—
the police had come to the hotel suspecting that
something was going on there but he had discour-
aged this search. None the less we felt it was time
to leave, but before we could do anything two rough
and brutal police entered demanding our papers. I
was uncertain of Raymond's cover story so I fumbled

and pretended to search, for I knew our British passports would give everything away, while I waited to
hear what he had to say. Perhaps it was Raymond
who thought of the ruse we employed, of snatching
their guns, clubbing them, and shutting the bodies
in a cupboard. Then we left.

Our only hope was to escape by plane, but if we
took an ordinary passenger plane they would want
to see our papers. However, private planes were to
be had at the airfield for a price, and Raymond knew
whom to contact. So as not to be seen, we dived
hastily past the open door of a room full of men
talking—obvious government employees. In the
room beyond, one small twisted figure with a bent
and paralysed hand—like that of my friend John
Hayward, who died the other day—was reading.
We got quietly into chairs so as to give an effect of
normality like that in the other room. Raymond
spoke of our wish to hire a plane, but for a long time
the man paid no attention. Then suddenly there was
action. He led us at a run past an airport gateway to
a helicopter. One of his men swung the propeller
too soon and was reprimanded. I climbed in first.
Raymond followed, then our pilot with the twisted
hand. We rose vertically and I saw the city spread
below us—we were safe.

IV

Statesmen and Politicians

For politeness' sake I prefer to make no distinction
between these two categories, for statesmen can also
be politicians. In the Common World I have met a
number of leading statesmen and with one excep-
tion (President Diem) I have liked them all—Ho
Chi Minh, Daniel Ortega, Allende, Fidel Castro,
President Mitterrand, and Gorbachev especially,
but few of these appear in the World of My Own.

Mr Wilson

When I encountered him first, in 1964, the Wilsons
had just finished dinner and the Prime Minister was
relaxing at his ease on a brass bedstead. He spoke
to me, as I thought, with an absurd hustings-air,
about his intention of cleaning the slums up with
one blow. I tried to prick his political manner.

'How will you house all the inhabitants?' I asked him. 'If this were the tropics perhaps you could put them into tents, but it is England and winter is approaching.'

'I shall lodge them temporarily in public buildings—town halls and the like.'

'Do you think they will be content? Now they have one lavatory between several families. Under your plan they will have one lavatory for hundreds.'

I don't remember his reply.

General de Gaulle

I have only a fleeting memory of de Gaulle, who during the Second World War in the Common World lived for a while in Berkhamsted, which was my birth place.

I was cutting up the bread ration and came to him with his share. 'Crust or crumb, *mon général*?' I asked him, but looking at the bread I saw how little was left of either. 'Better both,' I told him, and gave him all that was left.

Khrushchev

In the Common World I always felt a certain affection for Khrushchev in spite of his invasion of
Hungary. In the Cuban crisis I felt he had made a
favourable bargain with John F. Kennedy—no fur-
ther invasion in return for no defensive nuclear
weapons for Cuba, which in any case would have
reached no farther than Miami. I liked the way he
had slapped the table with his shoe at a meeting of
the United Nations. Perhaps I was influenced in my
affection by the meetings I had with him in My Own
World in 1964 and 1965.

My first meeting with him was at the Savoy, with a
group of Russians including Mr Tchaikovsky, whom
I had met in the Common World in Moscow when
he was editor of *Foreign Literature* magazine.
Khrushchev looked cheerful, healthy, and relaxed,
and he was only amused when two of his party dis-
puted noisily. We talked together about the method
of financing films in England and the bad influence
of the distributors. I said that this was one difficulty
the Russians did not suffer, but Khrushchev told
me that films in Russia were often delayed for six
months as a result of overspending and then waiting

for bureaucratic permission to increase the budget. He was very cordial and invited me to lunch the next day.

On the next occasion (for of the lunch I remember nothing) I sat next to him at dinner and he spoke no word to me until near the end, when he remarked that I had left a lot of my chicken uneaten. 'So much the better for the workers in the kitchen,' I said. 'Surely a Marxist believes in charity.'

'Not in Vatican charity,' he replied with a smile.

Perhaps he had that exchange in mind when we found ourselves sitting together again at dinner. It was a Friday and he glanced at my plate. I was eating beef. He commented with a smile, 'Meat on a Friday? I thought you were a Catholic.'

At our last meeting he was personally dealing with visas for the Soviet Union. He noticed that my profession was listed as 'writer', and he expressed the hope that I would write about his country. I noticed how very clear and blue his eyes were, and when I rejoined my friends I told them, 'When you see him close, he has a beautiful face, the face of a saint.'

My view of him, I found, was not universally shared in Moscow. One day I was in a crowd outside the

Kremlin. A podium had been raised and they were waiting for the leaders to appear. From another podium a young man began to address the crowd. He made fun of Khrushchev and mimed some anecdote of an international gathering at which Khrushchev had pulled roubles from his pocket and scattered them to show their uselessness.

It is a strange thing that sometimes that World of My Own seems to be influenced by the world we have in common. J.W. Dunne in his *Experiment with Time* might have argued that when I described Khrushchev as having the face of a saint (of a dead man) I had felt a presage of his dismissal, the news of which I learnt on the election-night broadcast of October 15, 1964, at the Savoy—where in the World of My Own we had dined together nine days before.

Omar Torrijos

On a visit to Panama I was surprised that Omar Torrijos, who had become a great friend, was absent, for he had made an appointment with me. When at last he came he was much changed. I had brought my daughter to act as translator, but he had learnt to speak a little English. With us was a very dull English soldier, General Denniston. Others joined

us—a number of Americans, including a comic soldier in an untidy uniform who lent me a tattered
volume of his published diary which I was not prepared to read. I was really there to warn Omar of an
American plot. The Americans intended to foment
disturbance with the idea of forcing him to leave
Panama. Panama would then, like an island in the
Caribbean, be used as a military base to blockade
Central America. I couldn't get Omar to understand
the plot.

Sir Alec Douglas-Home

In November 1965 I spent what I can only describe
as an unenjoyable weekend with Sir Alec Douglas-
Home, as he then was, at his house in Oxford. I
resented his smoothness, his Foreign Office manner, even his silk pyjamas (although they were almost indistinguishable from my own) and his silk
shirt, which was embroidered in pale blue 'Mar-
quess of Home', an odd inaccuracy. I had received
several messages from an Indian friend about radi-
cal riots in Allahabad which I showed him, and Sir
Alex strongly advised me against going to India as
'there's nothing to be done about that place.'

On my second night at his house I returned at
about four in the morning after dancing—an ex-

traordinary thing for me to do—at a small party. An old friend had tried to teach me to waltz and then less successfully to tango. When I returned to Home's house I found the lights on in his bedroom, and the manservant sweeping the floor. The chandelier had fallen and shattered.

'Lucky it didn't fall on your head,' I remarked.

'That goes without saying,' Sir Alec replied with a kind of cold satisfaction.

I went to rescue my pyjamas from the newly washed laundry that the manservant had hung out to dry, and in doing so (I don't really know how) I managed to get Sir Alec's pyjamas stuck up with Scotch tape.

Perhaps because of this I left the house and made my way towards Trinity College. At the corner of the Broad the rain came down in torrents. I must have lost my way, for I found myself in a kind of shell-hole surrounded by water. There seemed to be some soil a few feet away, but when Ralph Richardson, who happened to be nearby, offered to test the ground he disappeared below the water. I could see the top of his head several inches down. He emerged again complaining that it was very cold. I managed to jump onto the dry soil, however.

I walked on a little way and Sir Alec joined me. He must have heard me leave, but very soon we were both in a hole again. The situation was so strange that I began to make notes of what was happening, but the only paper available was in the form of white one-inch-square cards that Sir Alec carried. They seemed inadequate for writing, but apparently it was the custom to use them in the Foreign Office—perhaps a custom instituted by Lord Halifax, for I found his name in embossed letters on one of them.

All in all a weekend which I would prefer not to repeat.

Edward Heath

I once passed an agreeable evening with another prime minister, Edward Heath. Heath asked me about Chile and I described Salvador Allende to him and spoke of the good impression I had of the Communists in his government.

I lent Heath the typescript of a new novel I had written and he read it at intervals during the evening.

We went on to a pub and an old man spoke to Heath of his son who was in the army, and how he wished to have him at home for some family celebration. Heath introduced himself—rather quaintly, I thought—'I am the Right Honourable Edward Heath.' He asked for the son's military number, but the old man couldn't remember it. Heath told him to telephone his secretary the next day and everything would be arranged. To my surprise I found myself liking Heath very much.

Heath, it seemed, had been looking for an ambassador to Scotland, but no one wanted to accept the post. He even asked me and I refused. However when I read in the paper that no one else would accept, I went to him and told him I was ready to be appointed after all.

He looked exhausted and a little suspicious of me, so I explained that the only reason I had at first refused was that I felt incapable. But I would do my best. Perhaps as a mark of friendship we went swimming together in a muddy river, and to show keenness for my job I suggested we should hold a World Textile Fair in Scotland. He replied that David Selznick had once told him that such fairs might possibly do good in the long run, but that the last one had ruined many small local industries.

Yuri Andropov

It must have been about seven years after my meeting with Khrushchev that I encountered Yuri Andropov, at that time head of the KGB. He had recovered from his sickness and come to London on his way to Stockholm for a disarmament conference. He honoured me by making use of my services for note-taking. I liked him. He was an immensely tall man and there was something wrong with his right hand, which was apt to flap in a disconsolate way. I remember he told me of his great admiration for the poetry of A.E. Housman.

François Mitterrand

In December 1983 I had a brief encounter with President Mitterrand in London. He was walking to Paddington Station via Hyde Park. I told him how much I disliked Chirac and I would have added Giscard d'Estaing if Giscard had not joined us at that moment.

Fidel Castro

In June 1984 I was visiting Castro in Cuba. We walked around chatting in a friendly fashion and came to halt beside a poor man who was weeping. He had just buried a small child in a tiny grave he had dug himself.

Castro tried to comfort him by telling him that now his child would suffer nothing, know nothing.

But the man was not comforted. I crossed myself and he at once stopped crying and shook my hand. He said, 'I feel you are one of those who think there may possibly be something after death.'

Ho Chi Minh

Visiting President Ho Chi Minh, I found him very courteous, and he explained the difficulties which had made him refuse my previous visit. He took me for a walk in the countryside surrounding his HQ. One had to keep a weather-eye open for American bombers. A helicopter approached and I wondered whether it was American, but it proved to be one of 'ours' and landed. A very pretty European girl appeared and began to walk off on her own. 'Is she safe?' I asked Ho Chi Minh and he called after her, 'Come back. You don't know what our boys mightn't want to do with you.'

Oliver Cromwell

A lot of noise in the streets outside the flat where I was living—military commands, etc. It seemed very unusual. I tried to find out what was happening from the radio without success—it wasn't the hour for news. I went out and saw Oliver Cromwell walking down the street. I realized why he had once been described as the shadow cast by a crab. I had not expected to see him for at this moment they were voting in the army for and against his policy of executing Charles I. He sat down with a group of people and began to talk to them in French. He said Charles was in effect being killed by the doctrine of divine right. Without that a compromise would have been possible. News of the voting came—only an old officer had voted against Cromwell. 'He wants to shake the temple,' Cromwell said, 'but not destroy it. That would be fatal.'

V

War

I was visiting Berkhamsted when I learnt that, with
the permission of the British government, the United
States planned to drop four hundred parachutists
and take over the town at four A.M. in order to capture me. It was then nearly midnight and I tried
in vain to think of somewhere to go. I checked on
the time with two friendly police officers. One of
them questioned whether there might not be some
resistance.

'No,' I argued, 'they'll behave very well and probably bring balloons for the children.'

I went back to my room and was handling my
passport which would certainly betray me, when the
drop occurred early—at midnight. I found myself in
a room, under arrest. To the American plainclothes-
man in charge of me I said, 'When I get out of
here I'll have the pleasure of hitting you—I shall be
hitting a police officer for the first time.'

A voice behind me said, 'Do you really mean you've never hit a policeman before?' I looked around. It was my old friend Claud Cockburn, who was also under arrest.

We watched the American troops through the window. I had hoped they would disgrace themselves by looting and raping, but to my disappointment they seemed to be behaving correctly.

∽

In February 1965, after an air raid, German parachute troops landed in a quarter of London where I was living. With a friend I tried to get away by car, but I made the mistake of leaving behind a compromising letter dealing with espionage. As we drove away we passed two German soldiers who made no attempt to stop us. But a moment later we saw others approaching and we made another mistake by backing and turning, which aroused suspicion in the soldiers we had passed. We were arrested. Apparently they possessed a complete dossier on me, including a photograph taken with a concealed camera of my meeting in a hotel room with a German whose face I remembered from my trip down the Occupied Territories in 1924. They also appeared to have a tape recording of our voices. The game now seemed really up, and I felt almost resigned to the torture chamber, with an intellectual curiosity as to how long I would hold out. They possessed a radiogram of my body which would be of help to them.

∽

A full-scale German invasion started on June 23, 1965. They were moving into London from the south in a wide sweep. I and a friend, with one heavy gun—a mortar—between us, were operating as guerrillas on the flank. With our mortar we had attacked a German post and several hundred men and an officer had surrendered to us. Now we argued about our next move. Were the Germans aiming at London or did they intend to cut the road between London and the west? We decided to take a train, but we realized too late that it passed through German-held territory and we would be inspected.

A young German officer came up to see us. I stuck a revolver in his back and told him to go to the lavatory. There we intended to take his uniform. (Once before, my companion had escaped in this way.) But there was another German at the door and I could see from his look of triumph that he had pulled the emergency cord. The train stopped in a railway shed under blazing arc lights.

Suddenly I seemed detached from the situation and saw it as an observer. I was outside the shed and watched one man—my friend—dash out carrying our mortar. He found an empty cart with a huge cart-horse which reared up and leapt forward so that the car for a moment took to the air. Then a second man—surely myself—came out and ran after the cart.

∽

In 1966, only six months after the German invasion, civil war broke out. I was in my home town of Berkhamsted and, returning to the town after a walk on the Common, I found leaflets strewn around bearing what was obviously the code name for a military operation. I remembered what a close woman friend had said to me as a joke when I told her I was leaving England to live in France: 'You'll be back for the civil war.'

Near the station I saw in the sky a multitude of small planes and parachutes all the same colour as the leaflets, and as I hastened up Castle Street I found the parachutists were coming up behind me in a dense body filling the streets. It was some kind of an attempted Fascist take-over. A platoon of soldiers came down the road and a clash was inevitable because the Fascists would not give way, nor I hoped would the troops. But I was unprepared for the savage way in which the troops bayoneted the leading Fascists, for they were unarmed and it was a massacre.

I took refuge in a house where I found the Prime Minister, who was then Wilson. No one there seemed to want to know that fighting had started. Wilson appeared weak, worried, indeterminate. His only action was to go to another room to be left in peace.

∾

There was an occasion which I am proud to remember when I was instrumental in capturing Hitler. I happened to be waiting on a railway platform when I saw two men leave a train. One I knew was a general in German Intelligence, and when I looked at his companion I felt sure I recognized Hitler, though the absurd moustache had gone and his face was crumpled and more human. I shouted to all who were standing around, 'Hitler. Hitler's alive.'

The two men were descending into a subway. People looked at me as if I were mad, but I continued my cries and the escape of the two was stopped.

Hitler returned angrily to me. We went up to the end of the platform, where we sat down and talked a long while. I can't remember the subject of our conversation. A few others were there helping to guard him and presently a squad of soldiers arrived and took him away.

∽

Europe was under German occupation and I had an appointment for lunch with a leader of the Resistance who had been personally responsible for the murder of half a dozen German soldiers. 'I hope you don't sympathize with that,' a friend said to me.

I felt very conspicuous walking over a piece of open country in town clothes and a soft hat. German soldiers were drilling and a German officer was walking behind me. I was afraid of being stopped. I saw some militia also on an exercise.

At the entrance to a small town I was surprised to find a customs post. There was no avoiding it. I was stopped by a black soldier and the man in charge asked me if I had anything to declare. I said, 'Two hundred cigarettes.' He tore the pack open, checked the cigarettes, and returned them to me, pointing to a poster which authorized him to pass cigarettes if they were 'elegantly and properly' declared. So I went on to what I knew would be a dangerous lunch.

∽

I found myself back in the Malayan Emergency, which I had known in the Common World in 1951. I was hiding from the Chinese guerrillas, but at the same time I was a possible target for the British bombers searching them out. The bombers had an ingenious system by which electric lightbulbs lit up on the ground to expose the presence of a living person and then a bomb was dropped. I lay down on the ground and immediately a light went on beside me. I flung it away into the dark and crawled away, but as soon as I stopped another light went on. There seemed little hope of escaping the bombs, but all the same I somehow did escape, and joined an unofficial group of English who were searching for the guerrillas.

∽

I was only nine in the Common World when the First World War began, but in the World of My Own my memory of 1914 is very different.

The war began with total disaster to the British army and the unconditional surrender of Field Marshal French, who became himself a prisoner with another general who bore the name of Juillard. Their wives were allowed to join them in captivity, which helped their morale, and General Juillard's wife brought him an electrical apparatus with which he could 'do things' and pass the time. What puzzles me now is how we emerged victorious after such a total defeat.

&

For the first time in this very personal World of My Own I found myself someone else. I was Wilfred Owen, the poet, and I wore an officer's uniform and a steel helmet in the style of the First World War. I was alone in a dug-out and I recited a poem I had composed to the photograph of the girl I loved. I called the poem 'Givenchy', which I suppose was a place in the line held by my regiment. The poem went something like this and I spoke it aloud.

> *Imagine, dear, the shallow trench,*
> *An impregnable redoubt*
> *For this good night and more.*

Suddenly weariness of the interminable war swept over me and I began to sob. As I cried—or rather as Wilfred Owen cried—a voice said, 'The Germans have dropped gas bombs on this or that section.'

VI

*Moments of Danger
and Fear*

I have just spent a dangerous day in Haiti at Port-au-Prince. I was with my friend Trevor Wilson, a former member of M.I.6. whom I had last seen when he was consul in Hanoi. We were both arrested almost immediately on landing. My black police guard proved to be a great reader of rather juvenile fiction featuring a character called Bambi. Opening one of the stories at random I could see it was high-flown and erotic, with a scene where Bambi was being seduced by the Queen of Heaven.

I promised the man that I would get him the complete series of about seventeen volumes, and he whisked me into an invalid chair, put a cloth over my head, and so got me out of prison. Somehow I managed to release Trevor too and we went rapidly down the road and then up the drive of the British embassy to take refuge there. I was a little hurt by the coolness and lack of interest shown by the ambassador and his wife, who had just returned from a picnic. I had known them before, when they were in Santo Domingo. But of course ambassadors never want to get involved in trouble.

On another visit I had gone to the lavatory of my hotel in Haiti to shit when I was told that an admiral and a general were waiting to see me. I hurried to finish and join them. They looked a little absurd in their uniforms and decorations, but they seemed honest men. They told me that any day now there was going to be a revolution. 'You and your friends better get away as soon as possible. Anyway the moment you notice something unusual go into hiding. You have shoes—offer your shoes as a bribe. People want shoes badly and they would hide you.'

'What will you do?' I asked the general.

He replied with great dignity, 'I will die. No one will hide me.'

Rereading the diary I kept in the sixties of my life in a World of My Own, I seem to have played the same kind of Russian roulette that I once played in the Common World, for I returned yet again and again to Haiti.

In November 1966 I found myself driving very unwillingly through the streets of Port-au-Prince with

Peter Glenville, with whom in the Common World I had been working on the film of *The Comedians*, a book condemned by Papa Doc. Peter scented the danger which I felt myself in. There seemed to be a number of tourists about, and in a museum we encountered Seitz, the owner of the Oloffson Hotel, where I had stayed before writing *The Comedians*. While greeting Peter he turned his back on me. 'If you knew the trouble I have had,' he said, 'with the Tontons Macoute because of him.'

Upstairs I encountered two other people I had known—one a doctor. They were astonished to see me and more and more I wanted to get quickly away.

Out in the yard there were a number of cars. An old lady stood by a car close to ours. I had seen her before in the streets of Port-au-Prince. 'I believe that's Papa Doc's wife,' I said, and sure enough, the President himself joined her and they rode away. I tried to hide my face with my hand, and I was very afraid. Peter insisted on sitting quietly there at the wheel of his car eating a hard-boiled egg.

Finally when we did start we found the road from the museum blocked by a wooden post on a swivel. Peter got out to swing the post open, but just opposite was an armed sentry who said the barrier could not be raised without the President's order. This time we were really trapped. Luckily I remember no more.

૪

It was in 1972 that a lot of houses in London were destroyed by bombs. Going upstairs to my apartment with a friend I was immediately suspicious of a canister which was tied to a radiator on the stairs and attached by a glass tube to an electric point. My friend detached the tube and I went down into the street and showed it to a group of policemen.

One of them examined the tube and said there was enough explosive in it to blow up the whole block. They went into the house. I was afraid for all their lives, for a second bomb might have been planted, and sure enough a suitcase did explode and a shower of sharp little pieces flew in all directions— not dangerous but stinging.

૪

I found myself in a room where a parrot was at liberty and flew suddenly up to the ceiling. I explained to a companion who was with me, 'I am terrified of birds, as my mother was. I can't bear touching feathers. I can't stay in this room.' I went crouching into a little dark room next door, but the parrot swooped after me, nearly touching my face.

There were other creatures around me in this room, but they were little furry friendly ones. Suddenly someone thrust a large fat spider into my trousers and I felt it grasp my penis. This was worse even than the parrot.

∽

In January 1983 I was in Mexico attached to a gang of guerrillas pursued by the army. I and a companion had been separated from the main body. As we were crossing some rough country we were shot at from a line of shallow trenches.

My companion didn't reply but fired into the air, at which an elderly man who I think was his father stood up in the trench and waved his welcome. Then he ran forward and fell wounded on his knees.

Some time must have passed for the next thing I remember is the two of us, again alone, making our way along a road. Coming towards us were a man and a woman driving a horse and cart. I saw that the man had what looked like a very new rifle in front of him. As they reached us I grabbed the rifle and they passed out of sight round a bend in the road. I felt sure they would tell our pursuers where we were. My companion went back to the bend to see if they were close and he waved to me to make a deviation.

I could see that a company of troops was approaching, and when I looked down the road to my left where he had waved me to go I saw another troop marching towards us, while a third company was coming down the road towards me. We were hemmed in.

I decided to walk straight on carrying my rifle, and hoped they wouldn't recognize me. They began to pass without firing, but then I heard the click of bolts—they would shoot at any moment. The road we were on was striped alternatively white and black, and I thought—'White is life and black is death.'

I must have survived, for death is rare in dreams, so rare that I think I've only encountered my own death once—the death with which this book ends.

VII

A Touch of Religion

I am surprised to find how often religion of a kind
intrudes itself into the World of My Own. I write
'of a kind' for I have always resented being classed
as a Roman Catholic novelist. After all, one of
my books, *The Power and the Glory* (perhaps my
best), was condemned by the Holy Office, and the
Cardinal of Westminster previous to Cardinal Heenan severely criticized my work. I am not surprised
that in the World of My Own too I can hardly be
described as an orthodox Catholic.

Nevertheless, I have encountered three popes
there, though only two in the Common World—
Pius XII and Paul VI. Luckily John Paul II was
asleep when we first met in the World of My Own.

John Paul II is a great traveller and I am not sure in
what hotel and in what country we happened to
be staying at the same time. For a reason I don't

understand myself, for I have no liking for him, I felt a strong desire to make my confession to him. It was late evening and I hesitated a long while outside his bedroom door wondering whether to knock. Then I turned the handle and the door opened and there was the Pope in bed fast asleep. The face on the pillow had the same charismatic look I had seen on so many television screens. I stood looking down at it, wondering whether I should wake him, but there my memory fails me. I suppose I slunk away, carrying away with me unspoken what must have been a very unimportant confession.

My other encounters with Pope John Paul II have not been happy ones. In 1984 we had a walk together around the Vatican garden. He was in turn very amiable and then very impatient. We stopped beside two groups—one of women and one of men—who were playing cards. He gave a chocolate Perugina to each of the two winners, and I was a little disgusted by the pious and servile way in which they received them, as though he were giving them the Host.

In July 1987 I was shocked to learn from the newspapers that the same pope was thinking of canonizing Christ. I felt the man must be mad with pride to believe he was in a position to give an honour to Christ. As it happened he was on a visit to Antibes, and one day I passed him on the ramparts, kneeling in prayer and gazing at the sea. After I had passed I realized that he was following me and I slowed my steps, hoping that he might speak to me and that I would be able to express my feelings about the honour he was proposing to give. But he passed me without a word and turned off into the town. He was dressed in an old pair of very dirty white trousers and a green pullover. There was something pathetic in this disarray and for the first time I felt a little sorry for the Pope.

My only meeting with Pope John XXIII, whom I much admired, was a curious one. It occurred in the last year of his life. The Pope was blessing the sea, an ancient ceremony in the course of which he waded into the water waist deep, wearing his triple tiara. Unfortunately three unruly Englishmen were bathing at this spot and they combined together to splash the Pope. They were—I hesitate to give their names, but two of them at least are now dead— the Earl of Southampton, Sir Kenneth Clark, and Raymond Mortimer. Because I knew the last two personally, the Pope took me on one side when the ceremony was over and asked me to give them some form of rebuke, and he lent me a room in the Vatican for the purpose. I forget now, after twenty-four years, what I said to them, but I am sure I criticized them as strongly as I could, for their conduct had shocked me.

In the case of Paul VI, whom I had known and liked in the Common World, I remember a very different religious ceremony, but the handwriting in my diary after twenty-four years is sometimes difficult to read. A religious ceremony was certainly in progress, in Rome this time, before a great square palace which reminded me more of Vienna than of Rome, and did lions really play a part or is my writing deceptive? I seem to describe the lions who were there chasing after children, though I admit I was not sure whether it was a bit of flesh they were chasing or an innocent tuft of hair. There were also tall stone statues, with grotesque cardinals' heads, which moved around the square followed by a nun who beat them on the heads to prove that they were of stone. Finally, after all this, came Pope Paul's sermon—but it emerged from the throat of a mule of which I could see in mid-air only the head and the long extended throat, like a monstrous speaking-tube.

When I returned to the house where I was staying I found a jewelled crown on the dresser—presumably it belonged to the Pope—and I was tempted flippantly to try it on, but I feared that the Pope might enter at any moment.

I had on an earlier occasion been closer to Pope Paul VI than through the head of a mule. I found myself walking beside him in a procession up the aisle of a church in Rome. He seemed tired and dispirited and I began to tell him that he was working too hard and that we loved him (something I would never have said to his successor). Tears even came into my eyes. When we arrived before the altar there was an empty row of chairs for us to occupy. I felt that I had had more than I deserved of the Pope's company, so I hesitated to take the chair nearest him, but I was saved from that.

"Find a place for Saint Hugh," someone cried. Looking back over my shoulder I saw an old man with a white beard and a cheerful smile, and I gladly made room for him though I had no idea who Saint Hugh could be, for surely all saints are dead even in the World of My Own.

∽

Once I attended Mass with my mother in Crowborough, where my parents lived. We had found places in the front row. The priest was saying a Hail Mary in company with two servers. They made little steps towards the altar and halted between each line. I realized to my anger and disgust that the priest held a lighted cigarette in his hand, and so did one of the servers. At the end he turned to the congregation and said that soon a decision would be taken by Rome for or against the legend of the Virgin Birth, and that he wanted no trouble whatever the decision was. Then he walked down the aisle to greet the congregation as they left.

I was furious. I was determined, if I had the chance, to tell him what I thought of him. I slipped out and got to the door. He was busy talking to people. I hoped he would come to me, but I waited—I had the excuse of waiting for my mother. The priest returned into the church without speaking to me, and I followed him. He embraced a tall man, hanging as it were from his shoulders, and I found at last the courage to speak and told him how he had disgusted me. 'Couldn't you have waited for three minutes to smoke?' He smiled back at me in a superior and complacent way.

∽

Tonight at Mass a fat ungainly woman was helping the priest serve. She had plonked down a cup of tea on the altar beside the chalice, and this gave the impression that the priest was consecrating the tea as well as the wine. I felt very indignant and when Mass was over argued rather fiercely with the priest, who seemed a feeble and ignorant man.

∽

I have never liked lecturing, and I certainly do not feel competent to speak on religious subjects, but all the same I found myself on one occasion in My Own World explaining to a number of people my theory of the common evolution of God and Man, and the common identity of God and Satan.

This is how that theory appeared later in *The Honorary Consul*:

The God I believe in must be responsible for all the evil as well as for all the saints. He has to be a God made in our image with a night-side as well as a day-side. When you speak of the horror, Eduardo, you are speaking of the night-side of God. I believe the time will come when the night-side will wither away, like your communist state, Aquino, and we shall see only the simple daylight of the good God. You believe in evolution, Eduardo, even though sometimes whole generations of men slip backwards

to the beasts. It is a long struggle and a long suffering, evolution, and I believe God is suffering the
same evolution that we are, but perhaps with more
pain.*

෨

Someone was telling me that if I was visiting Israel
I should go to Emmaus, a small village that had not
changed at all since biblical times. It was there that
Joseph met Mary. 'But what brought him there,' I
asked, 'from Nazareth?'

'Perhaps,' the reply came, 'it was the same matter
of taxation which later took the two of them to
Bethlehem.'

෨

It was in January 1973 that I read in a newspaper
that I had been appointed Archbishop of Westminster. I was astonished and my feelings were some-
what ambiguous. I knew that I was quite unsuitable,

*In conversation with me, Graham Greene described how this passage
found its way into the novel from the dream, so for the interest of readers
I have added it here.* YVONNE CLOETTA

but all the same I was rather attracted by the idea of taking part in some royal occasion a few days later, with the Archbishop of Canterbury. I found that all the members of my family had been given two seats each for the ceremony.

I had been planning to leave London, but I told my mistress that I thought I should stay behind to get the robes and mitre and to learn, as it were, my part. I would have to be ordained as a priest first and for that I would have to consult my predecessor, Cardinal Heenan. Then whom should I run into but the cardinal himself?

He looked at me very sourly when I said that my appointment had come as a complete surprise. 'When it was announced,' he told me, 'it was a bombshell. I must talk things over with you.'

I went home with him. It seemed that he had asked a private detective to prepare a report on me. The report contained photographs, including shots in which the rather shabby and illiterate detective appeared with his witnesses.

'Who is Mrs Burton?' the cardinal asked. I replied that I didn't know the name. Perhaps the detective was referring to a woman who had been my mistress many years ago and was dead. 'He might at least have dug up someone more recent,' I said.

The cardinal had interviewed the Inland Revenue, who claimed that I had cheated on income tax by transferring money abroad. This did make me uneasy. Might they intend to reopen the case? His dossier also included a rather mysterious story of my trespassing in a field. After a lot of thought I remembered that I had once had the idea of moving into the country and had gone with my publisher to inspect a field in which it might be possible to build a house. The dossier became more and more absurd and farther and farther from the truth. By this time the cardinal and I were both laughing. He was relieved to feel that there was no longer any danger of my going ahead with the comedy of my ordination.

∽

Lying in bed, I made a great decision to turn my back on Christianity altogether and take up Buddhism. At that moment of decision I had the sense of Christ close by me. His outline was faintly visible in the dark, and he seemed unhappy at losing me. I regained at least my half faith.

∽

I had been reading an interesting Jewish book on Christ. It compared Christ's career with that of an earlier Jew called Mouskie. Mouskie had come to a very similar end. Jesus knew Mouskie's story and therefore he saw the likelihood that he would die in the same way. Mouskie too had foreseen his end, but his knowledge had been based on the Prophecies while Jesus's foresight was based on the history of Mouskie, which seemed to make Mouskie the greater figure.

Another interesting feature in the book dealt with the story of Nicodemus. He took refuge up a tree and refused to come down because he was afraid to speak to Jesus, since he saw that Jesus was guarded by two 'rough Galileans'.

∽

A new Order was being formed in the Church by a group of priests who were giving an exaggerated importance to Saint Paul, almost a priority over Christ. A symbol of the Order, which could be bought in shops selling pious objects, was a bust in china of Saint Paul with three arms, and heads growing out of his arms. I think the Order flourished best in Spain.

A reaction against the Order was being led by a priest I know, who had written a book criticizing it. Late one night he was rung up on the telephone by someone needing an urgent confession: a rendez-vous was agreed to at a church on the other side of town. He set out but slowly became suspicious. Was he being followed? He turned and went back.

On returning, he found the street in which he lived ablaze—not only his house but the houses of four other priests who had opposed the new Order.

∽

Archbishop David Mathew, who was an excellent novelist as well as an historian, was a good friend who saved me by his advice in our Common World from the attempted censorship of *The Power and the Glory* by the Holy Office. All the more strange do I find the account of his funeral in My Own World.

I attended David Mathew's funeral in December 1964. It was a very bizarre service. I sat in the gallery of the church with a friend and was much annoyed by the whispering, even giggling, which went on in the congregation below. I wanted to call down to them, 'The archbishop is my friend and he is dead.' Then my companion whispered to me, 'One of the priests—I do believe he's trying not to laugh.' It was very odd, and I might have put it down to the hysteria of grief had not another of the serving priests seized the altar by its end with a gay laugh a moment later and wheeled it quickly, like a table, out of the church. The service came to an end in a riot of gaiety.

Now, looking back after the passage of many years, I ask myself whether the end of life should not always be celebrated in some such way.

VIII

Brief Contacts with Royalty

King Leopold

One night in 1964 I was rung up by ex-King Leopold of the Belgians, who wanted my advice. He was organizing a fair to represent the history of Belgium, to be held in all the world capitals, and he was wondering how to deal with the unfortunate history of the Congo. I suggested that he should simply leave it out, but my reply satisfied neither of us.

I then proposed that he should be completely frank, and admit the crime of his great-great-grandfather (I wasn't quite sure that I had got the relation right) and the mistakes of the Belgian government. 'You might compare them with the crimes of other countries including my own—the massacre of Amritsar, for example.' I have never known whether he took my advice.

Queen Elizabeth

In 1966 there was a muddle about my reception at Buckingham Palace to receive the Companion of Honour. There had been a change of date and I was away in the Congo when the note came. For some reason my secretary lied and told the Palace that I had not received it. When I turned up for the changed appointment I was taken to one side by a state official.

'Tell me the truth,' he said. 'Your secretary lied, didn't she?'

'Yes,' I said. 'I can't imagine why. I was in the Congo.'

We passed by the Queen, who was sitting on her throne, and I paused to shake hands. She gave me a smile. 'Not yet,' she said, 'it would be a breach of protocol.' I had lost my place in the queue.

We went into the garden to pass the time. There were a lot of bishops about, and children sitting at tables eating buns and ice-cream. After an hour we went back in. I was feeling hungry and so, obviously, was the Queen, for she seated herself at the table and ate a bun. I was a little put out because she

called me by my original first name, Henry, which
I have always disliked.

It was two years earlier when, quite by chance, I
found myself sitting beside the Queen during a service in Windsor Chapel. The officiating clergyman
preached an absurd sermon and I found myself in
danger of laughing. So, I could see, was the Queen,
and she held the Order of Service in front of my
mouth to hide my smile. Then Prince Philip entered.
I was not surprised at all that he was wearing a
scoutmaster's uniform, but I resented having to surrender my chair to him. As I moved away the Queen
confided to me, 'I can't bear the way he smiles.'

King Ibn Saud

I encountered King Ibn Saud in a small by-street in
Westminster. He was wearing his robes and dark
glasses and had apparently just left his young mistress at a tobacconist's, where she lived over the
shop. I was impressed by the great courtesy he
showed her as he walked backwards to his taxi with
his eyes fixed on the windows of the upper room.

An Unknown Princess

I found myself in the company of a young Princess whose father the King was dying in a castle surrounded by watchers. Her life was endangered by his death. Suddenly there was a noise through the wall of his room, like a long whistle and then a sigh. 'That is the noise of dying,' I told her.

It was essential that the watchers should not know that the King had died, so immediately gay music began to be played within the castle.

I said, 'You must escape now, before the watchers know.' I tried to assemble the batteries for my electric torch, for it was dark outside, but the batteries were old and used up. 'Never mind,' I said, 'it's nearly day.'

I looked out of the narrow window and saw the watchers far below. It was essential to escape not only the watchers but the dwellers in the castle, and at least temporarily we succeeded. We found ourselves in a field of grass where there were the ruins of an old monastery. We walked through the ruins, but there were tourists there and I heard one say, 'Surely that's the Princess. I recognize her hair.'

I caught the Princess up outside the ruins and I told her we must get away as far as possible before someone reported us to the watchers. 'Take off your beret,' I said to her. 'They will say you are wearing a beret.' Presumably we escaped, for I remember no more.

IX

The Job of Writing

Writing plays only a small part in the World of My
Own. Once I came up with an idea for a short story
called 'The Geography of Conscience', about a
woman in Canada—an Irish Catholic who was going to rejoin her husband in Italy. She telephoned
to her bishop asking permission to use contraceptive
pills and he told her to follow her conscience, so she
took one. Then she found herself in Rome in a to-
tally different moral climate and she began to have
a bad conscience about the pills. The story was intended to be a comedy and it needed to have a third
twist of the geographical conscience. The idea seems
a possible one to me still, but I have never found in
the Common World the necessary third twist.

An idea for a novel also came to me. The scene was
a rather large, ruined old house, and the story would
pass from room to room, always avoiding the attic,

In the Attic

I doubt if I'll ever be able to buy well...

until the reader began to wonder what there was in the attic. Only in the last chapter would we see inside. The attic would be littered with scraps of old newspapers, and in putting these together the reader would finally discover what the novel was about.

The opening sentences of the story were all that made their way across into the Common World.

IN THE ATTIC

I doubt if the furnished flat which I had chosen to buy would have pleased anyone but myself. But as soon as the lift reached the top floor and I saw the cracks in the door, it was as though the flat held out a hand to me in welcome; it seemed to say, in a voice that creaked like itself, 'How good it is to see you here again.'

My few friends never understood my new friendship. All they saw was the decrepitude of my dwelling: hinges gone, cracks in the ceiling, a basin that leaked, a radiator that gave no heat. The state of the kitchen didn't trouble me, for most of the food I had enjoyed when I was young could now be bought in tins. I remember still the first night I spent there, and the dream I had. The dream, like all dreams, had many gaps, passages which memory has failed to retain. I sometimes wonder whether the memory is often a merciful censor, so that even a nightmare has been trimmed of the worst terror by the time we open our eyes.

§

As in the Common World, writing in the World of My Own has an almost nightmare side. On May 3, 1983, I started revising a typescript of my book *Getting to Know the General.* I found it impossibly bad. There were long, rambling sentences that led nowhere.

The next night I was working on my novel *Monsignor Quixote* and I realized that a whole long stretch of it was boring. I decided to amputate this whole section, but that would entail completely altering the end with the monsignor's death, and what other end could the book have?

§

In June 1965 I was rehearsing a play which I had adapted from a rather bad translation. My experience as actor-director was very similar to what I had experienced in 1964 in the World which was not My Own, when I was working on *Carving a Statue.* Peter Wood, who had directed that play, was now again directing, and Ralph Richardson was again playing the principal part with his usual flamboyant, false *bonhomie* and determination to get his own way. He continually wanted to revert to the old literal translation, which I had changed, and he had made his own marks in the text, which he didn't want me to see. There was one boastful moment when he put on his Edwardian-style hat, which was phosphorescent in the dark. I became more and more bored and irritated with the whole business. I told Wood how badly Richardson's part as 'the detective' was translated. He disagreed and I realized that my adaptation would soon, by agreement between himself and Richardson, be abandoned, so I told him that in two days I would leave for the South of France. There were no protests. I repeated, 'In two days— and I shall be happily lunching at the Colombe d'Or in St-Paul-de-Vence.'

∽

I had somehow against my will been persuaded to allow my suppressed novels, *The Name of Action* and *Rumour at Nightfall*, to be published. I had insisted on writing introductions to show my reasons for suppressing them and to demonstrate how bad they were. All the same, I was very worried and I imagined the fun the critics would have with them. I thought of forbidding any paperback edition, but apparently it was too late for that.

~

On May 5, 1973, I had an awful experience which I am thankful never occurred in the Common World. I had sent a love scene in a new novel to my secretary to make a draft, but her draft was full of gaps—that was only tiresome. What was awful was that, as I read the scene aloud to the woman I loved, I realized how false it was, how sentimental, how permissive in the wrong way. She too knew how bad it was and that made me angry. I threw it away. 'How can I read it to you,' I demanded, 'if you interrupt and criticize? It's only a draft, after all.'

But I knew that the whole book was hopeless. I said, 'If only I could die before the book is published. It's got to be published to earn money for the family.' The thought of Russian roulette came to me. Had I recently bought a revolver or was that a dream? My mistress tried to comfort me but it only made things worse.

X

Stage and Screen

A strange experience remains printed on my brain like a newspaper headline—'The Suicide of Charlie Chaplin'. It began with a rumour of my friend's death. I was in a great crowded cinema and I expected that at any moment an announcement would be made. I was even a little afraid of a panic among the audience at the news. However, later, the rumour was denied. A ring came at my flat door and when I opened it Charlie was assisted in. He really looked a dying man. Apparently he had taken poison but presumably not enough, and he made a gesture to indicate how much as he lay down. The poison had come from a tin. I asked his companion to give me the tin—'It might prove useful for me one day.' It was an ordeal to watch Charlie slowly dying, as I believed, but the situation suddenly changed —he recovered and was able to leave without assistance.

❧

In January 1984 I went to see a classic play called *The Game of Croquet*. I had a seat in the front row of the stalls and I felt a little nervous because a few days before in the opening scene Paul Scofield, who played the leading role, had inadvertently sliced a croquet ball into the stalls and blooded a spectator in one eye. However on this night nothing unfortunate happened. I found myself listening to a very interesting dialogue. The play was about three students who for final exams had to go to the house of an old academic and attend a party where each would be judged on his behaviour. One of the three was obviously very shy. The academic proved to be most friendly, and he seemed to be helping the shy one through his paces—helping him in fact to grow up and become adult. The dialogue ran easily and amusingly. I felt as though I were making it up myself.

❧

In May 1965 I was closely involved in the production of a blank-verse historical play with Richard

Burton and Elizabeth Taylor. I found them both more agreeable than I had expected, and Taylor more beautiful than I had thought, and a better actress.

The play was presented, for the first time, in the open air in Canterbury with the cathedral in the background. Burton made the opening speech before the appearance of a half-mad king—Henry VI?—played by my friend Alec Guinness. Guinness missed his cue and Burton covered up for him by improvising a verse referring to 'the recesses of this cavernous tent.' The audience laughed sympathetically when they realized what he was at, while Guinness looked around and said, 'I dried up.'

I was furious. I had the feeling he was behaving like this through jealousy of Burton, and I leant forward from my front seat and said, 'You swine.' He looked at me with injured surprise. Burton was unperturbed, but the performance for that night was off.

The opening was postponed till the following night. It was hoped that the critics would wait in Canterbury, but the next night the seats were all empty. Guinness played with his part in his hand, and although a television camera was there Burton treated the occasion like a rehearsal, interrupting the other players. A disaster!

᧖

Later in 1965 I was engaged in making a film with
Peter Glenville, from an original story set in Mexico
in the nineteenth century. Peter wanted to go riding
with me and he had found a small black horse for
me, but I don't care for riding and I let him practise
alone, riding in circles.

We arrived at the point in the script where an
innocent hero, Drew, in company of a man called
Houghton, is being pursued by sheriffs after a bank
robbery. They rest their horses for a moment by
one of those branching cacti known in Mexico as a
'candelabra'. Peter thought this presented an un-
necessary difficulty, but I assured him that making
a film about Mexico without showing a cactus was
like filming Paris without the Eiffel Tower. He
would only have to go a few miles south of Mexico
City before finding such cacti.

The character Drew would see the candelabra and
quote a nursery rhyme to Houghton, 'Here comes a
candle to light you to bed, and here comes a chopper
to chop off your head,' and at that moment the sheriffs' posse would appear on the horizon.

෨

I was asked to act the part of a priest who committed suicide at Mass, in a play to be performed in a small theatre in North Africa, but I was given no dialogue and the script gave no explanation of my actions.

I decided to extemporize.

A priest was preaching when I came on the scene. He told the audience that not only were the consecrated water and wine holy, but also 'the implements' of the Mass, the chalice and paten. I called out that I didn't care a damn about these objects. 'I am a priest and I am killing myself, God, because you have ceased to love me.'

Next day I went into the town and asked two Africans if I had succeeded in shocking the audience. They assured me that the people were very shocked indeed, and were still talking about it. Incidentally, they told me that Saint Augustine had lived in this town.

෨

I was taking a walk in the West End with Randolph Churchill when he suggested that I help him to write a film script about his father. The danger, I told him, was banality. I had an idea for an original treatment of the subject, with the title *A Great Man.* The story would be about minor fictitious characters, showing how their lives were changed by certain emotional points in Churchill's life—VE Day, for example, and his last sickness. He liked the idea and told me he would try to get the Queen's co-operation.

ഗ

I was commissioned to direct a film of one of Ibsen's plays, and I had done no homework. I had thought of no camera angles, cuts, etc. Ralph Richardson was to star in it, and someone had warned me that he intended to get me sacked and humiliated on the first day.

It was Richardson who introduced me to the *équipe* — about twenty men sitting at long tables, having refreshments. I made the mistake of apologizing for my inexperience and they shouted back their mocking agreement. If only I could get through the first day's shooting, I thought, I'd be able to study the play at night.

A remark of Ralph's gave me a clue. 'I want to begin,' I said, 'with an exterior shot of your monocle lying on a doorstep. We pan up and see you cursing from a window above—whatever curses you are in the habit of using.'

But after that promising beginning we began to quarrel. He talked of appealing to his agent. 'Are you threatening me?' I said.

'Yes. I am.'

'I shan't appeal to anyone,' I told him. 'I shall cut your face open with a riding whip.'

∽

I had been reading a play about Everyman for stage production. At a certain moment he makes his great decision to destroy the world with the help of a nuclear bomb. I felt the scene should be produced more or less on these lines: The moment of his decision must not be melodramatic; it should take the form of quiet and banal dialogue—something the audience would hardly notice—but for the sake of theatrical effect there must be a long pause after the simple lines, and then a great lighting effect, perhaps taking the form of the shadow of an enormous bird.

∽

Carol Reed told me that Peter Ustinov wanted him to direct *King Lear* on the stage. Ustinov would play King Lear. I felt doubtful whether he would be suitable, though there were parts where I thought he might be very good—as in the scene on the blasted heath.

I was in bed while we were discussing this and Carol warned me that Ustinov was going to bring me my breakfast. He arrived with a sheet over his head, which he removed when he had put down the tray. He had grown a snow-white beard, and it had transformed his face into something gentle, saintly, even sentimental. He began to recite the long passage in which I had thought he would be at his worst—'Pray you, undo this button.' To my surprise he was excellent.

∽

I was in a very confused state in 1973 about a play I had written rather in the line of *The Potting Shed*. Peter Glenville had criticized it very severely and I began to rewrite it. I quite realized its faults. There was a scene where the principal male character knelt and made a long prayer. I altered the stage direction to indicate that he sat on the edge of his bath, and prepared to cut the prayer drastically, but to my surprise it was only two lines long. Suddenly I realized that the play was very short, and with an exhilarating sense of creativity I began to add lines, and a new scene right at the end.

XI

Travel

I have travelled as much, I believe, in the World of My Own as I have in the Common World. My travels in both have not been without drama, but in My Own World one travels at the speed of the fastest jet.

West Africa

I seemed to have only just embarked, in 1965, when I found myself in Sierra Leone—no longer the colonial country I had known and grown to love during the war, but part of independent Africa—where my young daughter was on trial for her life. She had been heard to criticize the President.

There seemed to be no defence counsel to cross-examine witnesses, and I couldn't understand the tribal language they spoke. Was it Temne? Was it Kru? Was it Iguazu? One man strode across the court making an oration which he interrupted to shake my hand. I recognized him. I remembered how, more than twenty years before, I had cracked his skull with a stone, but he bore no malice. We liked each other. He was a chief and his name was Tumba and I wished he could be in charge of the country.

During an adjournment I sought in vain to find a solicitor. I wished to appeal to the judge and tell him that my daughter had only been in the country for a few hours; anything she had said she must have learnt from me, and I wished to take her place in the dock. All must have ended happily, for my daughter is very much alive.

Arabia

Sometime in the 1960s I was cruising at night off some point of Arabia. In the interior not far away was the ruined castle of Orbutum. There were stories that somewhere along this coast were the lost mines of King Solomon. Mysterious lights shone in the sky above the castle, and there was a legend that, if you named someone you had loved, a light would fall and indicate where the treasure lay. I whispered a name (a Swedish name) but nothing happened—was it perhaps that I had not loved enough?

None the less, I persuaded the captain that we should search in the ruins. We had to take out permits for our hunt, guaranteeing to keep no more than one percent of what we found. That was no matter in the captain's view—they would never know what the correct percentage was. But before we could start our hunt, an American naval officer arrived who claimed sole rights. We told him we had priority, but he indicated that that meant nothing. In his papers it was printed that the American government kept the castle of Orbutum in repair for tourists, and in return the government had the first right to prospect. There was no arguing with the American government.

China

In November 1964 I was lucky enough to have an interview with the Emperor of China, in the city which I still prefer to call Peking. I was travelling with my friend Michael Meyer, the translator and biographer of Ibsen, but he proved a poor travelling companion as he continually suffered from headaches and other small ailments.

I was dressed unsuitably in a sports shirt, and I began to apologize to the Emperor for my informal attire. The Emperor surprised me. He half ran, half slid into the room, a thin elderly man dressed in a black-tailed suit but without the tie. He was followed by some high mandarins in traditional dress, and after a few words they took us driving in the streets of Peking. At one moment the Emperor inexplicably left us, and a moment later we heard him calling from behind. We had not time to turn our taxi before he reached us in another taxi and transferred back to our car.

I was tired of the streets and walls of Peking and suggested for the sake of Michael, who had never been in China before, that we might see a little of the country outside. 'I remember among the rice fields a small green village around a temple, very beautiful.'

The Emperor left us again and one old mandarin asked about my previous visit. I wanted to show him some lovely photographs in colour which I had taken, but I found in my pocketbook only grey sad photos of naked starving people (and a few of police violence which I shuffled hastily away). I couldn't help showing him the others, but I tried to minimize the effect by localizing it in place and time. 'They were taken,' I said, 'that year when there were bad droughts in Kyoto.'

Syria

It was in June 1965 that I found myself in Syria
during a horrible massacre of children, even babies.
I had seen something rather like it once in Damas-
cus on a feast day, but not on this scale. I was one
of a party and I thought it unwise to go out in the
streets, but I was overruled—there was said to be no
danger for foreigners. Men were going around with
knives, and later, when we were sitting at dinner, a
woman came in with a baby on a platter, and she
sliced it in half as you open a bag.

Australia

In July of the same year I was travelling through
Australia, a country I had never known in the Common World except for one day in Sydney. My car
had got sunk in a stream and four men helped me
to lift it out. I felt grateful until one of them started
talking of the cost of 'salvage'. He said that I owed
them between eighty pounds and a hundred and
twenty pounds. He was a real bully and I felt scared
of him. In the end I paid out the eighty pounds. He
took it grudgingly. He obviously hated the English.

Graham Greene

I knew that I couldn't continue to live in such a
country.

Liberia

I seem to have been travelling a great deal in 1965,
for two weeks after Australia I found myself in Liberia on a visit for the *Sunday Times*. It was more than
thirty years since I had walked through Liberia with
my cousin Barbara in the world I share with others.
A great deal had changed in Monrovia, the capital.
I found myself in what could truthfully be called a
luxury hotel. My purpose was to interview various
members of the government, and I asked someone
how I could set about this. 'Nothing easier,' he told
me. 'Leave it to your secretary. She'll manage.' And
manage she did. I found I had a rendezvous arranged with nearly everyone except the President—
and I was very glad not to see him, for he had every
reason to hate me, since he was Doctor Duvalier,
late of Haiti, Papa Doc.

The same month found me again in West Africa,
where there was a dangerous situation with some
villagers who were enraged against the whites. It
was suggested that someone unarmed should go in
and talk to them. Not without some fear, I volun-

teered. I joined another man and we went in together. Someone had questioned my qualifications
and I replied that I had always liked Africans. The
situation was tense in the village, but all passed off
well. As we left, we met a group of nuns who were
only too pleased to see us.

The U.S.S.R.

I was walking with four companions through Moscow at night, but a KGB car frightened my friends
and they left me alone. I thought it best to go up to
the KGB officers of my own accord and ask the way
to the Europa Hotel. The officers said, 'Get in the
car. We'll take you there.' At the hotel someone
brought a high-chair for the second officer, and I
could see now that he was a dwarf. I asked him why
people were not allowed in the streets at night. He
replied, 'We want the streets to be safe.' I said, 'Safe
for whom, if nobody's allowed in them?' He admitted that I had a point there he hadn't thought of.

Cuba

I was taken by car across a frontier to Havana. In a
bureau there I spoke to a member of the govern-

ment. My friend who had brought me assumed I would now be given a car and would travel south, but I was getting tired of the Cuban revolution, and unwilling to take risks. The minister as usual was quite unco-operative. My friend said that all the priests had left and the countryside was in the hands of the suffragettes—magnificent-looking women, but what horrors! I told the minister that I had written much in favour of the revolution, but I had had no help at all from his side. He said evasively, 'You have seen more than we have.' 'What do you mean?' 'None of us has seen a priest drunk.' He was referring to a character in my last article—a priest I had seen in an aeroplane when I was returning home.

South Africa

While I was in South Africa I read an account in an Afrikaans newspaper of a police interrogation which I had suffered. Everybody sympathized with me. I took off my left glove to show a rather twisted hand, but I refused to accuse the police of torture. 'They were just angry at my answers,' I said. I felt rather proud of my generous attitude, but at the same time secretly pleased at being regarded as a hero. 'It was a woman who twisted your fingers, wasn't it?' 'To tell you the truth, I only remember two men. Perhaps there was a woman there. I seem to remember very little of what happened.' I thought I would try to send a message to my friend Etienne Leroux, a novelist I admired, to say that I was in Cape Town, but I didn't want to get him into trouble so I thought I would use the name Verdant, which he might recognize as Greene.

XII

Reading

I had just been reading with great pleasure (and I had marked many passages) a new translation of the Bible by my friend George Brown, the Labour politician. I liked particularly his treatment of the Psalms, which had always bored me. George had left only stray fragments of them, so that they gave some of the intriguing interest we feel for the scraps of a mutilated papyrus.

❦

In reading Boswell I came across this remark by Samuel Johnson, which I found amusing. It concerned farting.

'The Canons kept the wind under their robes until the smell could be attributed to the ladies, or else

the ladies had waited until the wind could be attributed to the Canons.'

※

A crowded party, everyone helping themselves to
food and drink. I joined Claud Cockburn, who was
talking to a young writer with the surname Graham.
They were discussing George Orwell. I said that
1984 was a bad novel, like all his novels. It was only
his essays which were good.

※

A Jesuit priest called Blunden wanted to talk to me
about a criticism I had made of the Pope. When we
met I asked him if he was a relation of my friend
the poet Edmund Blunden. He said, 'No,' and made
a derogatory remark about his poetry. He said Blunden had run out of steam.

I replied that that happened to everyone with age,
and he had left a fine body of work behind him. He
admitted that 'The Midnight Skaters' was a good
poem, and I tried to remember the title of another
which ended with the line 'Look up with hatred

through the glass.' I started glancing through a collection of his, but I couldn't identify the poem.

∽

Somebody had shown me a book by Sacheverell Sitwell in which he claimed that he and his wife had gone to live in Kenya because of something I had written about him. They were suffering from intense loneliness but couldn't make up their minds to return. One terrible and true phrase sticks in my memory: 'Loneliness is not shared with another—it is multiplied.'

∽

To my astonishment my publisher, Frere of Heinemann, began to praise the novels of C.P. Snow. He said they had a world-wide reputation. I denied this. In France, I said, he was practically unknown, and I began to point out the absurdities of his style. There was a character in the book Frere was reading who 'had' or 'took' his wife. However, I couldn't shake his inexplicable admiration.

∽

I wanted to read certain poems from Robert Louis Stevenson's *A Child's Garden of Verses* to my small son (no longer small in that Common World we share). I couldn't find the collected poems, which had been edited by Janet Adam Smith, although I knew I had a copy both in Antibes and in Paris. All I could find was a selection with very bad illustrations, and it left out all the poems I liked (including the one I wanted to read, which contained the line 'a sin without pardon'). My son was pleased with the illustrations, which made me all the more disappointed not to find the poem. I at last, but too late, after he had gone, found the edition I wanted tucked away in a cupboard.

∽

With a French friend I had been wandering through Paris. Only in retrospect do I realize what a Victorian Paris it still is. We came to a kind of market with second-hand bookshops on the periphery, and in the centre people engaged in the manufacture of books:

stalls where type was being set, stalls where books were being bound. In the first second-hand stall I stopped at, I saw with delight bundles of old *Strand* magazines tied with string. Nothing was in very good condition, but all the same it was a shop after my own heart. Mixed in with one bundle was a Nelson sevenpenny—I think by Booth Tarkington—but not one I wanted. However, I found a Dick Donovan for my collection of Victorian detective stories, and another detective story by an author unknown to me, but to my great disappointment the bookseller told me that his stock was for lending only. I continued round the market, but the other stalls contained mainly reference books.

∽

In My Own World recently my mother read poetry to me—poems I had liked when a boy and perhaps neglected since, for they now seemed to take on a new quality. One poem was by Robert Bridges: 'Whither, O splendid ship, thy white sails crowding. . . .'

XIII

Science

A Nobel Prize Winner

I had been reading a very interesting book written by a woman doctor who thought she had found a cure for a fatal disease of the intestines caused by a virus known as Fugger. She injected a wasp with Fugger—from which she was suffering herself— and induced it to sting her on the stomach. She was cured. She consulted a medical friend who asked her whether she really believed in the cure, and she admitted she was only a half-believer. However, he encouraged her to continue her research. Two patients were cured, the third died, but then a fourth was cured. She was awarded a Nobel Prize for medicine, but then two more patients died. The doctor friend suggested that the cure depended on the psychology of the patient and the degree of his or her belief. She was depressed by the bad results and her own half-belief. Her husband volunteered to help her by being injected with Fugger and treated by the wasp sting. His heroic act was rewarded—he was cured.

Outer Space

A friend showed me two objects which had fallen from the sky through his roof. One was a ball of rock which might have been a natural product; the other was a beautifully fashioned skull in a white substance like marble. This could only have been carved by an intelligence resembling the human. It really seemed a proof of intelligent being existing in outer space.

Studying the moon's surface through binoculars, I suddenly discovered a human face carved on a great crag. I was immensely excited by this discovery and all that it suggested, but I couldn't get anyone else to see it.

XIV

Love?

I spent a sad summer evening in July 1965. I was
engaged to be married to a girl whose mother de-
tested me and longed to see the affair at an end.
Harassed nerves caused a quarrel between me and
the girl and her pride added its quota, while I pushed
the quarrel to its extreme so that the girl broke with
me and I accepted the break. The mother listened
with satisfaction and then took the girl upstairs.

I felt sad and guilty and I knew that my relief at
this final solution would not last. A party was going
on at the house and the mother reappeared with her
daughter in her arms, small and shrunken and ready
to vomit. The mother appealed to me to find something and I brought a vase into which the girl vom-
ited. I felt pity and guilt and love too, and I realized
for the first time how much she loved me and what
I was losing.

Among the guests was Henry Moore, and as I

left the room I apologized to him for not having recognized him earlier, as I had been so preoccupied with my quarrel. I left the house and went for a walk with the girl's brother. He was very sympathetic to both of us. We met her father, whom I had always liked, and appealed to him. 'I am not such a rotten beast, am I?' He smiled to reassure me.

When I got back to the house the girl was there, and everything was all right again between us.

XV

A Small Revenge

A small revenge is as sweet in My Own World as it is in the world we share, and all the more when it comes unexpectedly, as it did during the afternoon of November 20, 1988.

My sister Elisabeth had called on me unexpectedly with a friend just as I was leaving my Paris flat and I invited them for a drink in a usually quiet bistro round the corner. There were more people seated there than usual, and I was hesitating whether to stay when Elisabeth spoke sharply to a man sitting apart who seemed to be writing notes. 'Do you always wear spectacles?' she asked him.

'No,' he replied with some astonishment.

'Would you take them off?'

He obeyed and my sister said, 'Oh yes, I thought I knew you.' She explained to me, 'He's a lawyer who's been against you in about four libel actions.'

'Did he win them?'

'Never more than a few hundred pounds.'

Everybody in the bar was listening attentively.

'You are Mr Creen?' the man asked.

'My name is Greene,' I told him, 'not Creen. But I suppose you would think both names were a Screen.'

XVI

My Life of Crime

I found myself concerned with a woman in a murder. We had concealed the body in a railway truck—a porter passing in one direction could not see it, but to others it was still visible. We began to make our getaway, but looking back I saw that a crowd had gathered.

At the entrance to the station there was a control, but we passed safely through. Then again at the exit from the station yard there was another control, and a small queue had formed. The guard was on the telephone, probably being warned about the murder. I managed to push my way through, but my companion was held up.

I walked rapidly down the street and took the first turning that came. It led to another station and here I was rejoined by my companion. She had struggled successfully with the guard. I told her that the best thing for us was to take the first available train anywhere. One was just beginning to move and we scrambled on without a ticket, but we bought tickets from the collector, and found the train was bound for somewhere on the Marne.

'It's a grim grey region,' my friend said.

'Never mind,' I replied. 'If we had stayed in Paris they would have only one place to search. Now on the Marne they will have ten thousand places to look, and we shall be on the way to the east.'

Unfortunately, just behind us in the carriage was an inquisitive couple, and the man had been reading a newspaper which contained an account of the murder. My friend was wearing a very distinctive pointed cap and I feared it might appear in a photograph in the paper. I told her to take it off and I held it scrumpled up on my knees.

Our fellow traveller continued with his questions. I told him we were writing a story together—a story about some criminals. Well, hardly criminals. There was no question of a big crime. It was a tale about a troop of *jongleurs* who stole venison and cooked it on stolen wood.

∽

I was living in a small room with my mistress and I was wanted by the police in connection with a robbery. Some of the stolen things were concealed in the room. Looking through the window, I saw the police gathering for a raid. I was determined to fight capture but suddenly the room was full of tiny birds with blue wings—they flew back and forth like a shoal of fish. When they began to settle on my shoulders my first reaction was fear and abhorrence, for I have always been afraid of a bird's touch, but then my fear went. I could feel them against my neck as soft as a kitten. My whole mood changed. Love came in place of fear and defiance, and when the police broke in I made no resistance. They allowed me to walk behind them to where other prisoners were gathered. We were put into a Black Maria and during the trip one of the prisoners attacked a guard with his handcuffs. I held him back.

§

In May 1965 I stole something of great value, although it looked like no more than a scrap of black lace. If it was discovered I would suffer a long term of imprisonment. A plainclothes policewoman came to search my apartment. She was quite sympathetic but very thorough. I kept the scrap in my hand for a long time, but I feared that eventually I would be searched myself. When she was occupied with something else I hid it in a carton of lump sugar, pushing it under the lumps. Unfortunately she finally reached the point of opening the carton and peering inside. I hoped it would be too dark in the carton for her to see a scrap of black. She looked for a long time and then closed the box. The search was at an end.

I asked her if the police would now be satisfied that there was nothing in my apartment and she agreed, but I didn't quite trust them not to make a sudden return visit and I tried to think of a better hiding-place. Perhaps I had learnt my lesson, for in the twenty or more years that followed I find no reference to another theft.

XVII

Unpleasant Experiences

I had a very unpleasant experience. I found *crevettes* were coming out of my penis with my urine. There were about twelve in the lavatory bowl, and one *langoustine*.

∽

There I was sitting in my favourite small restaurant with this old tart in her sixties. What had ever induced me to pick her up—pity? I talked to her politely. She didn't look like a tart, I thought, and hoped again. I heard my name mentioned at a neighbouring table and tried in vain to hear what they were saying about me. She expected me to go home with her after this, and what was I to do? I was stupid enough to tell her that this was my favourite restaurant. I thought: I won't be able to come here for months in case she looks for me here.

For some reason we left the restaurant separately, and I thought for a moment of creeping round the corner, but I decided that would be unfair and unkind, and then I heard her 'coo-ee'. I explained to her as well as I could that there simply wasn't time to go home with her that afternoon, and that anyway I was too tired. In that case, she said, I'd have time to look in at an exhibition of religious art in the church at the end of the street. I agreed though I had no intention of going, and I pressed a hundred-franc note into her hand.

XVIII

Animals Who Talk

It is one of the charms in this World of My Own that animals talk as intelligibly as human beings. For example, on the evening of October 18, 1964, I was caressing a tabby kitten who boasted to me in a small clear voice that she had killed four birds that day. I rebuked her with pretended anger since I am not very fond of birds. She replied with a certain pathos, 'But you know, I got forty-two francs for them.'

$\sim$

I was worried and a little frightened by a beastly little yapping dog who resented me coming into the house. When I turned my back on him I could hear him making dashes at my heels. I shook my finger at him and scolded him and he collapsed on his side and whimpered out, 'Are you going to punish me?'

I replied, 'I damned well am.' He made a little pool of spittle in his fear.

~

In a hut by the sea where I was living I received a visit from a remarkably intelligent dog. I had met him once before, with his owner. He had close, curly black hair. He opened the door himself and came and laid his head upon my knee. He asked wistfully, 'Am I faster than Diamond?' Diamond was a cat. I said, 'Yes.'

'Am I faster than. . . .' He mentioned an old spaniel.

'Yes,' I said, 'but remember he's very old.'

Later I had to reprove him for putting his paw on the table laid for two and stretching it towards the sugar basin. I tapped his paw gently and he left the room, opening the door himself and closing it behind him.

~

In Milan with my friend Yvonne and her setter dog, Sandy. Yvonne went into the cathedral and, when I looked around for Sandy, a bystander told me he had followed her in. But this was not true—it was a different dog. Sandy was lost, and we were about to leave Milan. I went round all the side streets, calling his name with increasing anxiety. At last someone said, 'Here he is,' and a setter bounded towards me with enthusiasm. Only when I had brought him back to the hotel did I realize he was of the wrong colour. So back I went calling 'Sandy!' and to my relief he came. He said to me, 'If only I had carried a handbag with a little money for a taxi. I was lost, and I didn't even know the name of the hotel.'

XIX

Disease and Death

I had to have a massage for the back. The masseur—
who seemed to be American—found two black spots
on my buttocks at the base of the spine. He said he
had to get them out, and pinched one very hard
while giving me a running commentary. It hurt quite
a lot before he was successful with the first. I looked
over my shoulder, expecting to see nothing longer
than a match head, but he was holding a large
scampi wrapped in a transparent caul.

'Is it alive?' I asked.

'Sure it's alive,' he said.

'I would have thought that I would feel it eating
away at me.'

The masseur was hot from his exertion and
mopped his brow. 'It doesn't eat you. It's like a vege-
table. It sort of lies in you, as though it were in the
earth.'

He began to work on the second one. This was

even more difficult. He said, 'They can give you hepatitis. Maybe I've saved you from that in time.'

He gave an angry exclamation. I think he had broken off the head of the second one, leaving the body in the flesh.

∽

My mother had died and her dead body had to be lifted from a bed and carried into another house. I didn't want to help, but I had to, and I didn't want to look, but it was necessary. The body was very thin and dry and shrunken. It was easier to move it in a standing position, and at moments it resembled my elder sister, who had died many years before.

Then I heard the body speak as I moved it. It said, 'Cold. Cold.' I tried to convince the others that the body could not really be dead, but they paid no attention. I told the body that I would light a fire and soon it would be warm. There was no reply, but I felt a horrifying pity. One could suffer after death, it seemed.

∽

I had a discussion about the fear of extinction by death. I began by telling of a dream of mine which suggested to me that there was an afterlife for those who believed in it. In the dream I had been aware of people I had loved who called to me to join them. But I had chosen, by my lack of belief, extinction. A great black cone like a candle extinguisher was to be dropped over my head.

In the discussion that followed, I argued that we all, whatever our beliefs, feared extinction.

∽

In this World of My Own I found myself writing a bit of verse for a competition in a magazine called *Time and Tide*, but, needless to say, the paper never received it. It was about my own death.

> *From the room next door*
> *The TV talks to me*
> *Of sickness, nettlerash, and herbal tea.*
> *My breath is folded up*
> *Like sheets in lavender.*
> *The end for me*
> *Arrives like nursery tea.*

DEMCO